MY 1ST GRAPHIC NOVEL

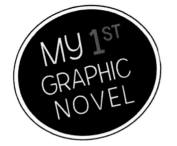

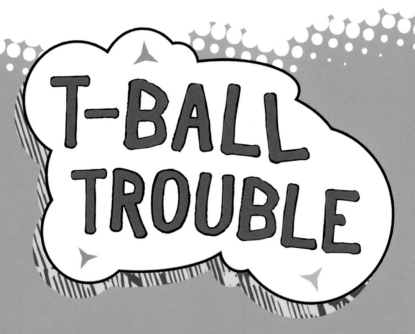

T-BALL TROUBLE

My First Graphic Novels are published by Stone Arch Books
A Capstone Imprint
151 Good Counsel Drive, P.O. Box 669
Mankato, Minnesota 56002
www.capstonepub.com

Library of Congress Cataloging-in-Publication Data
Meister, Cari.
    T-ball trouble / by Cari Meister ; illustrated by Jannie Ho.
    p. cm. — (My first graphic novel)
    ISBN 978-1-4342-1300-6 (library binding)
    ISBN 978-1-4342-1413-3 (pbk.)
    1. Graphic novels. [1. Graphic novels. 2. T-ball—Fiction.] I. Ho, Jannie, ill. II. Title.
PZ7.7.M45Taam 2009
741.5'973—dc22   2008031973

Summary: Marco wants to play baseball, but he's too young. Instead, he joins a
T-ball team. He gets lots of new equipment, but is he ready to hit off the tee?

Art Director: Heather Kindseth
Graphic Designer: Hilary Wacholz

Printed in the United States of America in Stevens Point, Wisconsin
010654R

T-BALL TROUBLE

by Cari Meister
illustrated by Jannie Ho

STONE ARCH BOOKS
www.stonearchbooks.com

HOW TO READ A GRAPHIC NOVEL

Graphic novels are easy to read. Boxes called panels show you how to follow the story. Look at the panels from left to right and top to bottom.

Read the word boxes and word balloons from left to right as well. Don't forget the sound and action words in the pictures.

The pictures and the words work together to tell the whole story.

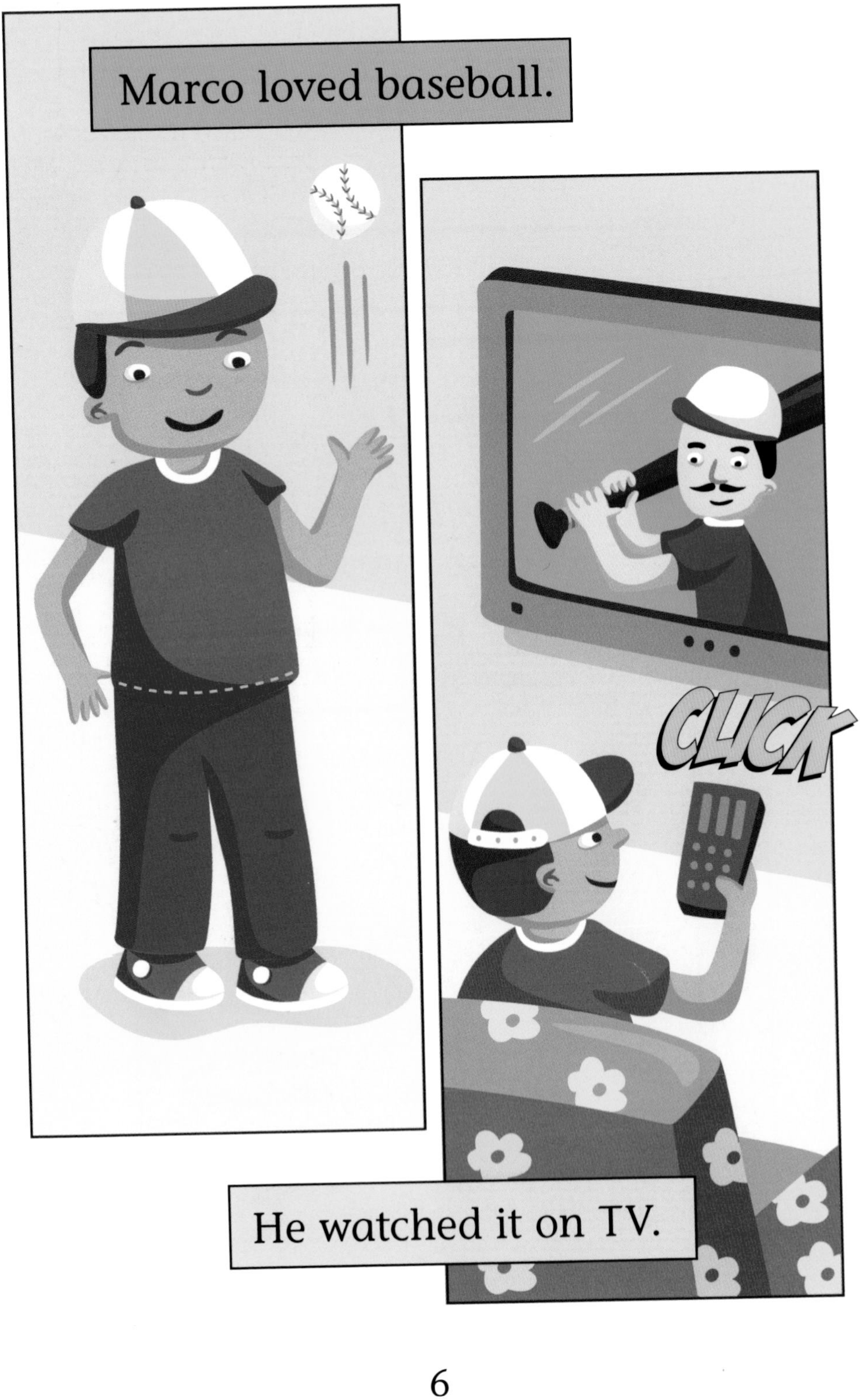
Marco loved baseball.
CLICK
He watched it on TV.

He watched his older brother. He watched the kids at the park.

Marco wanted to play baseball, too. But he was too young.

Marco got a hat and a jersey.

Marco also got a bat.

Marco practiced at home.

He hit the ball off the tee.

Sometimes he hit the tee.

Sometimes he hit the ball.

11

Marco practiced with his team.

They practiced throwing.

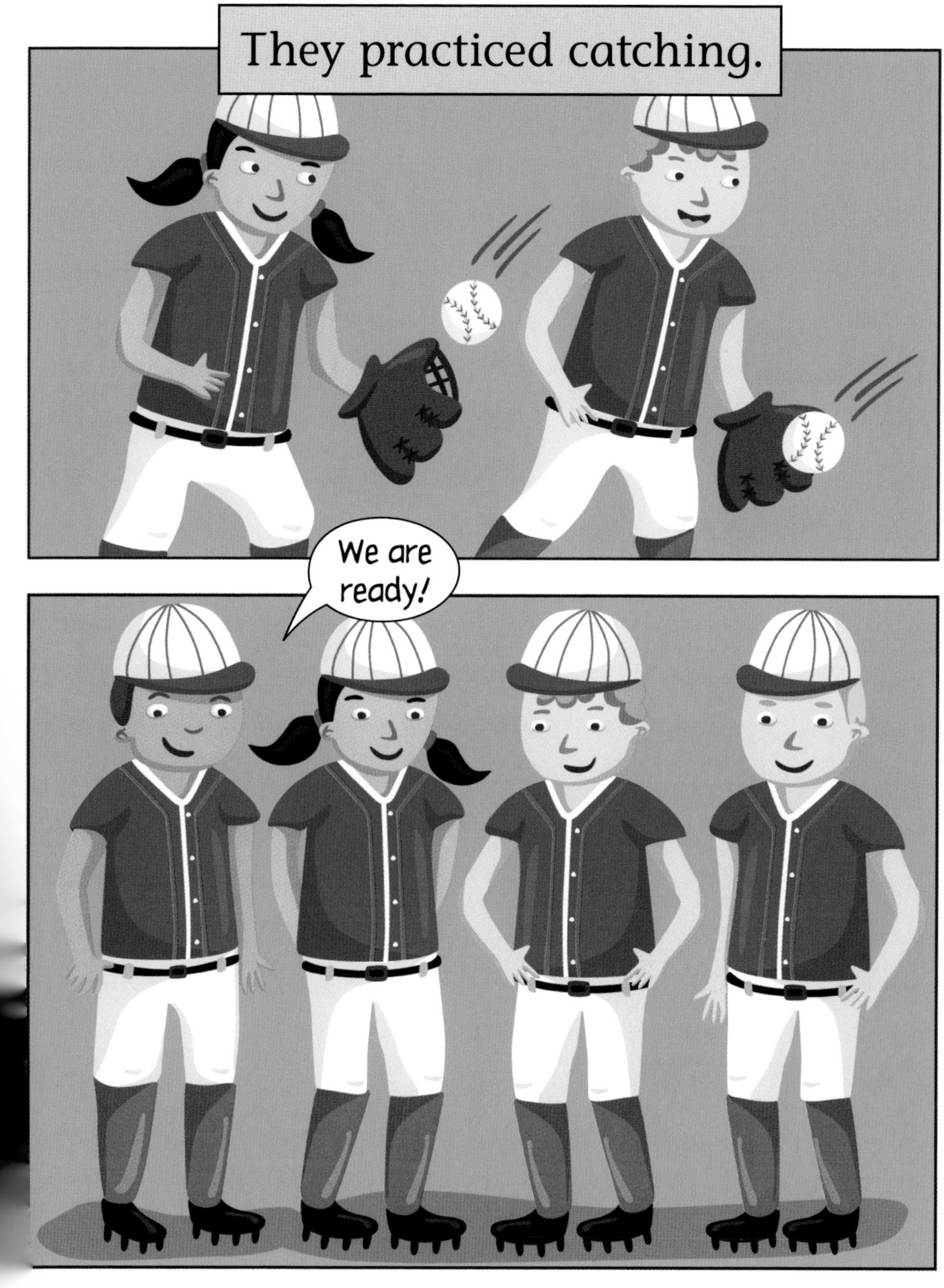
They practiced catching.
We are ready!

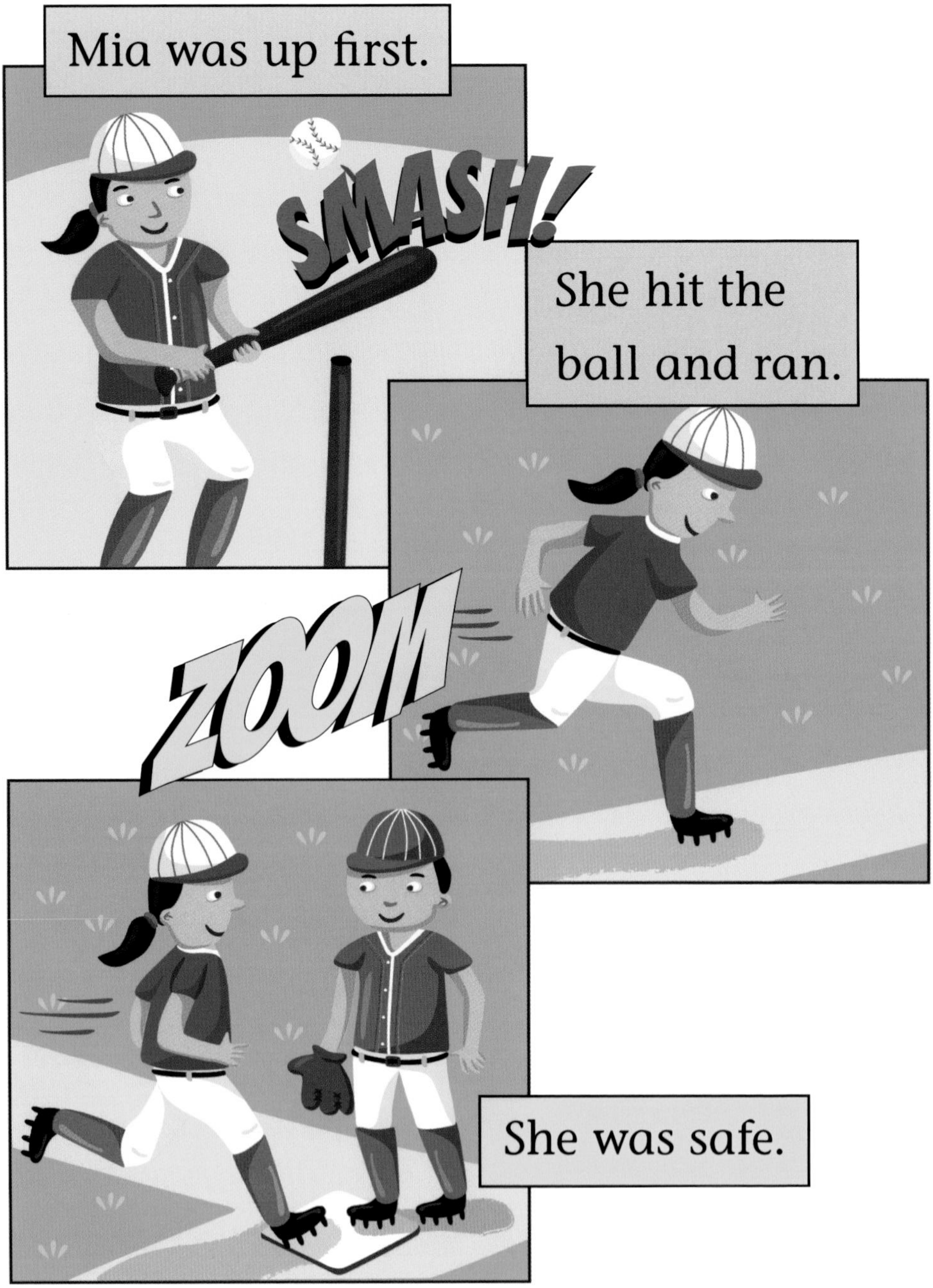
Mia was up first.
SMASH!
She hit the ball and ran.
ZOOM
She was safe.

Evan was next.

He hit the ball and ran.

He was out.

But Mia made it to second base.

It was Marco's turn. He ran to the tee.

He swung.

He hit the ball.

It went on the wrong side of the white line.

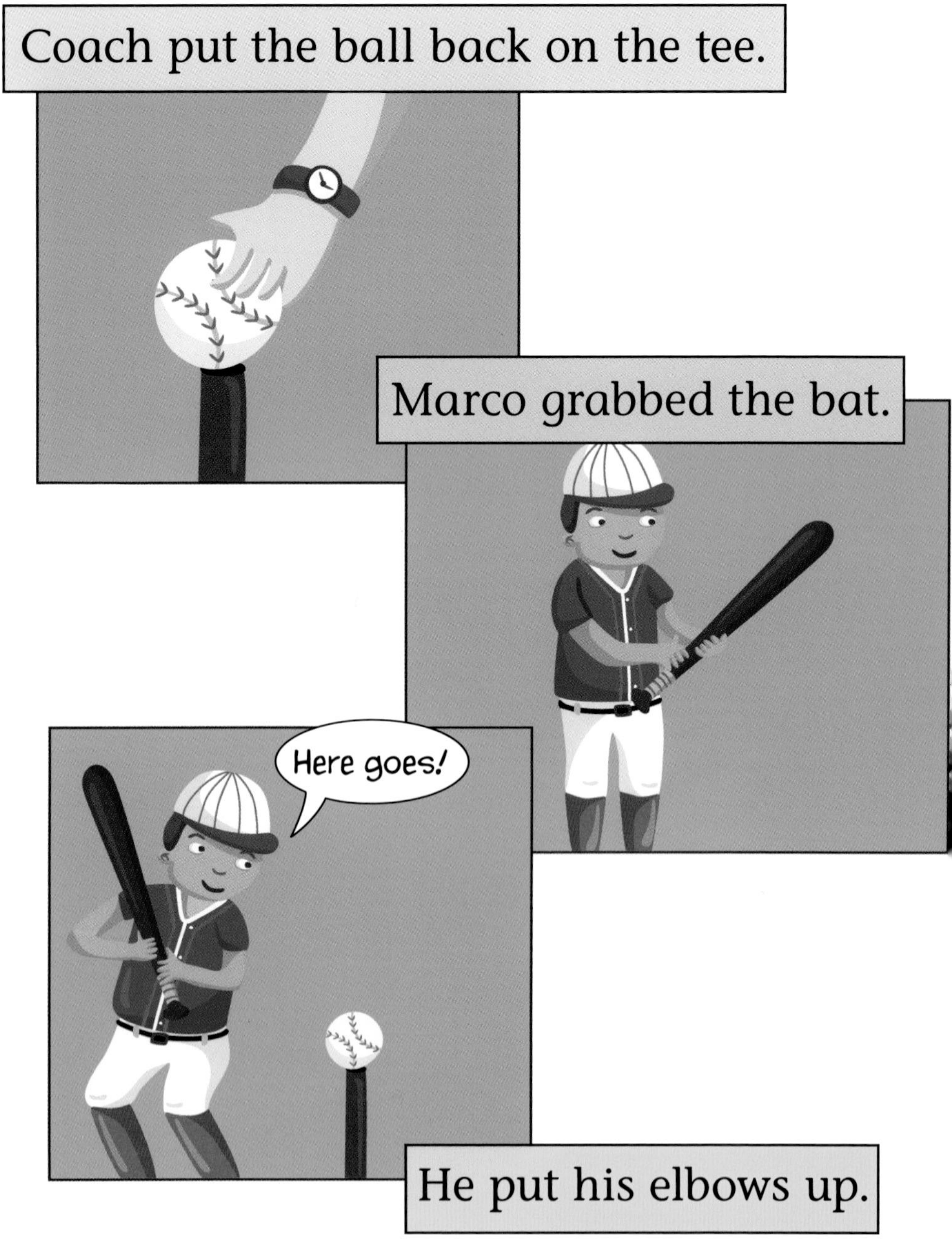
Coach put the ball back on the tee.
Marco grabbed the bat.
Here goes!
He put his elbows up.

He bent his knees.

He swung.

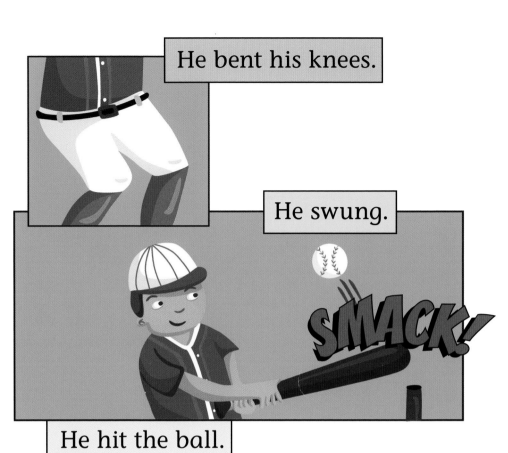

He hit the ball.

It went far! It was foul again.

Marco hit the ball three more times.

Coach talked to Marco.

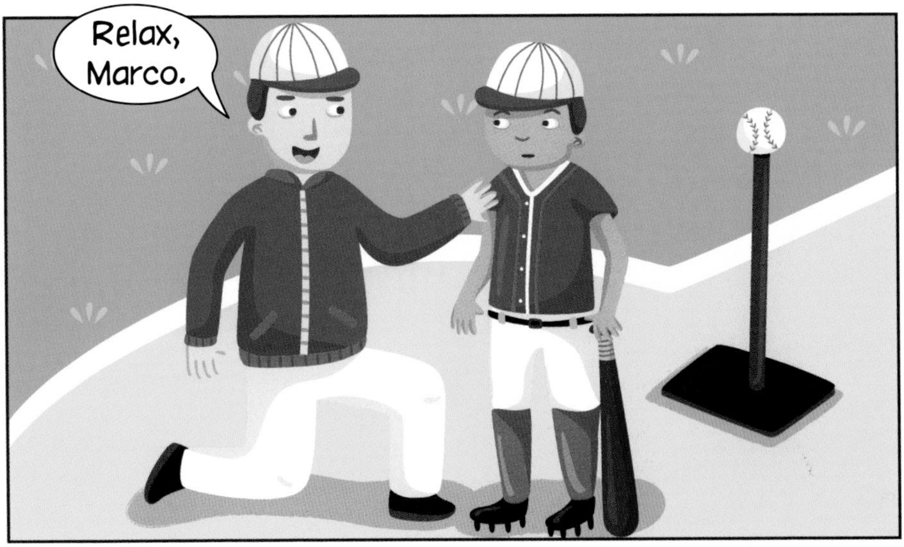
Relax, Marco.

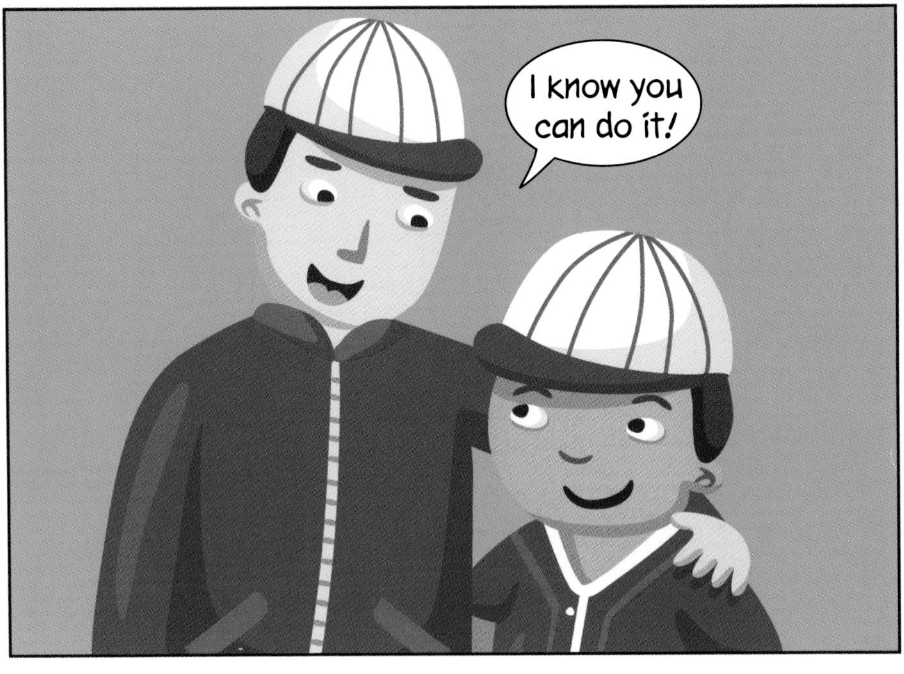
I know you can do it!

Marco held his bat just right.

He swung.

He hit the ball.

The ball soared in the air.

It was not foul! Marco made it to second base.

Mia ran home and scored.

Go, Mía!

Marco's team lost the game, but they were proud.

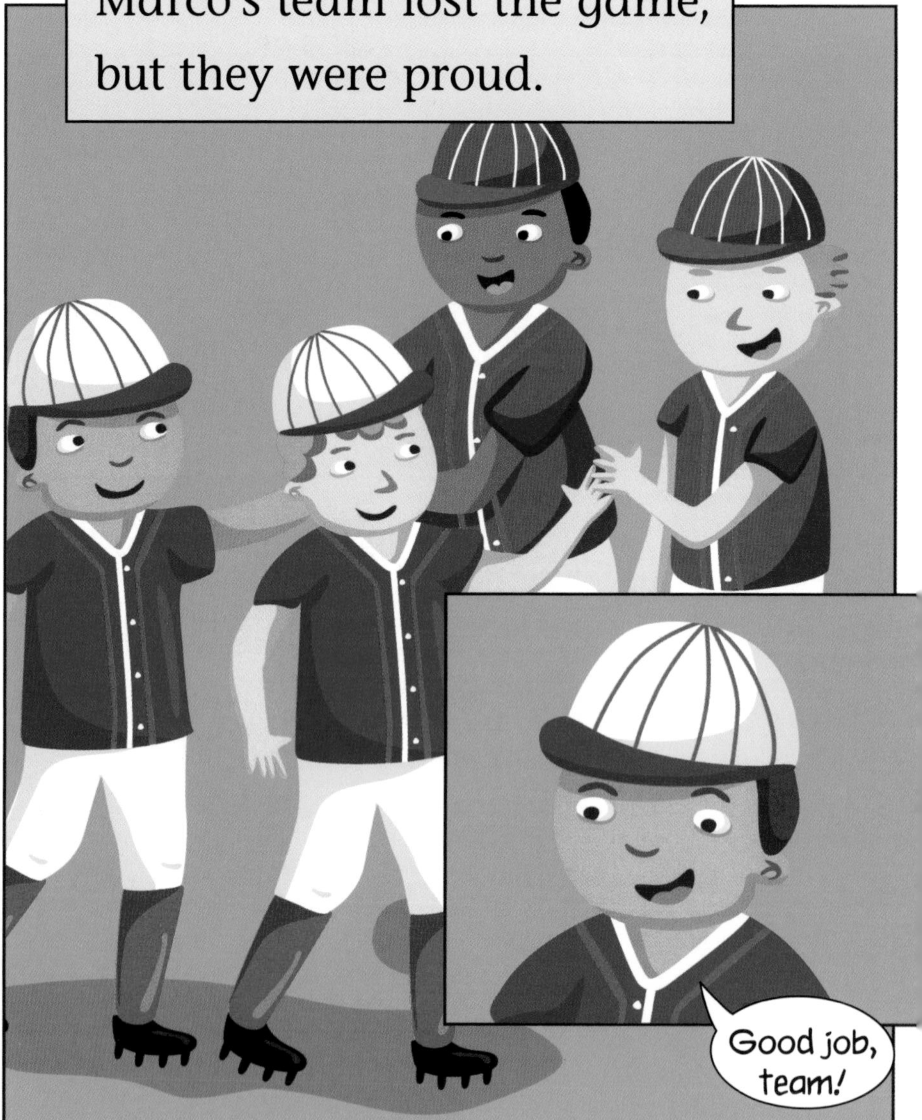
Good job, team!

They tried hard and had fun.

The End

ABOUT THE AUTHOR

Cari Meister is the author of many books for children, including the My Pony Jack series and *Luther's Halloween*. She lives on a small farm in Minnesota with her husband, four sons, three horses, one dog, and one cat. Cari enjoys running, snowshoeing, horseback riding, and yoga. She loves to visit libraries and schools.

ABOUT THE ILLUSTRATOR

Born in Hong Kong and raised in Philadelphia, Jannie Ho studied illustration at Parsons School of Design in New York. Jannie has been drawing ever since she can remember. Much of Jannie's work and style has been inspired by Japanese and retro art.

GLOSSARY

foul (foul)—out of bounds

jersey (JUR-zee)—a shirt that is part of a baseball uniform

practice (PRAK-tiss)—to do something over and over

tee (tee)—the post that the ball is put on in T-ball

DISCUSSION QUESTIONS

1.) Have your parents ever told you that you were too young to participate in something? If so, what was it?

2.) The coach knew Marco could hit the ball. He believed in him. Name a person who believes in you. Explain what they do to show you they care.

3.) Marco's team didn't win the game. But they were still happy. Discuss a time that you didn't win but were still proud.

WRITING PROMPTS

1.) Marco liked to watch baseball. What's your favorite sport to watch? Draw a picture of your favorite team.

2.) Marco and his friends practiced catching, throwing, and hitting. Write down at least three things that you practice.

3.) Throughout the book, there are sound and action words next to some of the art. Pick at least two of those words. Then write your own sentences using those words.

THE FIRST STEP INTO GRAPHIC NOVELS

My FIRST Graphic Novel

These books are the perfect introduction to the world of safe, appealing graphic novels. Each story uses familiar topics, repeating patterns, and core vocabulary words appropriate for a beginning reader. Combine the entertaining story with comic book panels, exciting action elements, and bright colors and a safe graphic novel is born.

WHAM!
My FIRST Graphic Novel
GOALKEEPER GOOF
by Cari Meister
illustrated by Cori Doerrfeld
SPORTS FICTION
RST Graphic Novel
RAH-RAH RUBY!
by Christianne C. Jones
illustrated by Cori Doerrfeld
SPORTS FICTION
My FIRST Graphic Novel
THE END ZONE
by Lori Mortensen
illustrated by Mary Sullivan
SPORTS FICTION
My FIRST Graphic Novel
T-BALL TROUBLE
by Cari Meister
illustrated by Jannie Ho
SPORTS FICTION

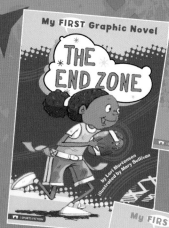

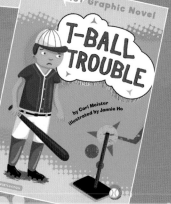